This Little Hippo
book belongs to:

Scholastic Children's Books,
Commonwealth House, 1-19 New Oxford Street,
London WC1A 1NU, UK
a division of Scholastic Ltd

London - New York - Toronto - Sydney - Auckland
Mexico City - New Delhi - Hong Kong

First published by Scholastic Ltd, 1999

Developed from the
original books by Michelle Cartlidge.
Story adapted by Caryn Jenner. Illustrated by Colin Twinn.
2 4 6 8 10 9 7 5 3 1

ISBN 0 590 11375 5

Printed in China

Michelle Cartlidge's

TEDDY TRUCKS

The Great Key Chase

Little Hippo

The Teddy Truck drivers were cleaning their trucks. Nutley the dog watched, as Jacko's keys jingled and jangled on his belt.

"My truck is so clean, I can see my face," said Gerry.

Jacko looked at Gerry's reflection and laughed. His keys jingled and jangled.

Suddenly, Nutley grabbed the keys in his mouth.

"Nutley, give me those keys!" called Jacko.

In the Teddy Trucks office,
Boss Bear was thinking.
  "We need jobs from the
town's top teddies," he said.
  BRRRING! BRRRING!
  "Hello?" Dusty answered the
telephone. "It's Mayor Bear,"
she whispered.

Boss Bear picked up the telephone. "Good morning, Mayor. You have a job for Teddy Trucks? Yes, I know you are the town's top teddy. You can depend on Teddy Trucks. Don't worry. I'll send out the drivers right away!"

"Nutley!" Jacko called, as the dog ran round in circles with his keys.

The other drivers laughed.

"He's your dog, Gerry," said Jacko. "Train him."

"Nutley, sit," Gerry said.

Nutley paid no attention.

"Nutley, can you run round and round?" Gerry asked.

Nutley was already running round and round.

"You see, he's a very good dog," laughed Gerry.

"Boss Bear to TT3," came the voice over the radio. "Come in, Jacko."

Jacko tried to catch his breath. "Yes, Boss?" he said into the radio.

"I've got an important job for you and Gerry."

While Jacko listened to Boss Bear's instructions, Nutley ran off with his keys.

"Nutley!" called Gerry.

Nutley climbed onto the shed and dropped Jacko's keys on the roof.

Gerry and Jacko followed.

"Woof!" barked Nutley.

He jumped down, leaving
the keys on the shed roof.
  "Now I'll get my keys back,"
said Jacko.

A mischievous jackdaw saw the keys shining in the sunlight.

"Leave those keys alone," Jacko told him. "We've got an important job."

But the jackdaw picked up the keys and flew off.

"After him!" called Jacko.

Jacko and Gerry raced after the jackdaw. They followed it to the park. The jackdaw perched in a tree, with Jacko's keys still in its beak.

"Nice birdie," said Jacko.
"Squawk!" said the jackdaw,
and flew away.
"Come back with my keys!"
called Jacko.

The jackdaw dropped the keys on the grass.

"There they are!" said Jacko with relief.

He was about to step on the grass, when the park-keeper stopped him.

PLEASE KEEP OFF THE GRASS

PARK KEEPER

"Haven't you read the sign?" he asked. "Look."

Jacko and Gerry looked at the sign. It said: *Please keep off the grass.*

"Now what shall we do?" asked Jacko.

21

"I have an idea!" said Gerry.
They borrowed a fishing rod
from a teddy who was fishing
in the pond. Jacko cast the
fishing line over the grass and
hooked the bunch of keys.

PLEASE KEEP
OFF THE GRASS

"I'll soon have those keys back," Jacko declared.

He flicked the fishing line. It flew over his head towards the pond.

PLOP! The keys splashed into the water.

"Oh no!" Jacko groaned.
He handed the fishing rod to Gerry, then dived into the pond. Gerry began to reel in the line. The keys dangled at the end of it.
"All right!" called Jacko. "I can get them now."

PLEASE KEEP OFF THE GRASS

24

Jacko grabbed the keys from the fishing rod, accidentally giving it a tug.

Gerry was still holding the other end of the rod.

"Don't pull, Jacko!" shouted Gerry, but he lost his balance and fell into the pond.

Together, Gerry and Jacko
went to Rosie's Café to dry off.
   "Well, at least I got my keys
back," said Jacko.
   "Here's something to warm
you up," said Rosie, and she
gave them each a steaming
hot bowl of soup.

OPEN

They were about to tuck in, when Bella and Wilson walked into the café.

Suddenly, Jacko jumped up. "I've just remembered!"

Gerry jumped up, too. "Boss Bear's important job!"

They dashed for the door.

Bella and Wilson sat down at the table.

"We've just done Boss Bear's important job," said Wilson.

"Yes, and Mayor Bear was delighted," added Bella.

Wilson took a spoonful of soup. "Mmm, delicious."
Jacko and Gerry sighed. What a day!
"Sit down, you two," Rosie laughed. "I'll get more soup."

NO TABLE SERVICE